CONTENTS

NODDY™
ANNUAL 2007

Pedigree®

Published by Pedigree Books Limited
Beech Hill House, Walnut Gardens, Exeter, Devon EX4 4DH.
E-mail books@pedigreegroup.co.uk
Published 2006

£7.99

WELCOME TO TOYLAND

Hello, everyone!

My name is Noddy and I think that I am the best driver in the world! Martha Monkey says I'm wrong, so I have borrowed Mr Sparks' tow-truck to prove that I can drive *anything* with wheels. You can read all about my driving adventures later! Lots of other things have been going on in Toy Town, too: we've had trouble with the Town Hall clock, it was Mr Wobbly Man's birthday, Big-Ears' magic rubber went missing and Master Tubby Bear caused all kinds of mischief with it! Before you find out more, come and meet my Toy Town friends…

NODDY'S CAR

I really do think of my little red and yellow taxi as a friend. When I talk to my car, it answers with a friendly 'Parp! Parp!' of its horn. Driving is such fun, too, so I enjoy taking passengers around Toy Town in it!

TESSIE BEAR AND BUMPY DOG

Tessie Bear, Bumpy Dog and I love to go for picnics together when I have a spare hour or two. Bumpy Dog is very bouncy, but he's clever, too: you can read about how he showed me the way back to Toy Town when I got a little lost!

BIG-EARS

Big-Ears lives in Toadstool House in Toadstool Wood. He's my best friend and he is very wise indeed. He is kind, too: whenever my car is being mended, he will take me around on his bicycle. I usually buy him a Googleberry Surprise as a big thank-you!

MR. SPARKS

Although he spends most of his time running Toy Town garage and fixing cars, Mr Sparks can mend anything at all – even the big Town Hall clock. I thought his garage might be a good place to live once, but it was far too noisy!

MARTHA MONKEY

My monkey friend Martha thinks that anything I can do, she can do better! I love to prove her wrong; it makes up for all the naughty tricks she plays on me. I like to have little competitions with her, but one thing I won't let her do is drive my aeroplane!

MR. WOBBLY MAN

It must be such hard work wobbling all day long. We had a lovely birthday party for Mr Wobbly Man, but what he really wanted to do was lie back and look at the clouds. You will see later how we made his wish come true!

MISS PINK CAT

The Ice Cream Parlour in Toy Town is famous for its delicious ice creams and creamy milk shakes. Its owner, Miss Pink Cat, asked me to be her driver and I found out what she was really like. You'll soon find out, too!

MR. PLOD

Our town policeman is Mr Plod. Sometimes he can seem a little stern, but he always lets us know that he is there to help us. He might even let me borrow his bicycle to show Martha Monkey what a good cyclist I am, too!

SLY AND GOBBO

Sly and Gobbo are two naughty goblins. Gobbo is the clever one and comes up with mischievous plans, while Sly is happy to help carry them out. How delighted do you think they were to get their hands on a magic rubber? Read the story to find out!

9

WELCOME TO TOYLAND

Hello, my name's Noddy
And I live in Toy Town.
Come and be my passenger,
Climb in! I'll show you round.

That is Toy Town garage.
Hello there, Mr Sparks!
Through the square…there's Bumpy Dog,
He's seen me – how he barks!

Up there's the Town Hall clock,
It's not quite all it seems…
That's Miss Pink Cat's Parlour;
She sells the best ice creams!

There's a naughty goblin,
I'll bet he's played a trick!
That noise from Toy Town station's
The Express – it's really quick!

The jail, the pond, the market,
I think we're almost done.
Shall we stop here for some tea?
This is my House-For-One!

JUST IN TIME FOR TEA

Noddy has come to see his friend Tessie Bear. He is just in time for some tea and freshly-baked cakes. Use your crayons or pencils to colour the picture and make the cakes extra yummy!

DON'T BE LATE, NODDY!

Noddy was having a little rest from taking passengers around Toy Town. He decided to go for a picnic in the Toyland countryside with Tessie Bear. The two friends chatted and ate lunch while Bumpy Dog dashed to and fro nearby, enjoying all the open space.

"Woof! Woof!" barked Bumpy Dog, bounding up to Noddy. "Do you want to play fetch, Bumpy?" asked Noddy, picking up a stick. "Go and get it then!" Noddy threw the stick and Bumpy Dog chased after it excitedly. "He likes that game," giggled Tessie Bear.

Bumpy Dog trotted back to Noddy and whimpered. He could not find his stick! "Don't give up, Bumpy Dog," Noddy told him. "Noddy's right," agreed Tessie Bear. "If at first you don't succeed, try and try again. You must keep looking until you find your stick."

Bumpy Dog scampered off and was soon back with his stick. "Look, Noddy, he found it," said Tessie Bear. "Good boy, Bumpy!" smiled Noddy. His smile then turned to a frown as he heard the Toyland Express approaching. "Oh, no!" he cried, jumping up.

Noddy hurriedly packed away the picnic things. "Noddy, whatever's the matter?" asked Tessie. "I didn't know it was so late," Noddy replied. "I'm supposed to be waiting at Toy Town Station for Mrs Skittle when that train arrives. Come on, we must be quick!"

Noddy, Tessie Bear and Bumpy Dog set off for Toy Town. They had not gone far before they came across a newly fallen tree on the road. "Oh, no!" cried Noddy. "We'll never get back in time!" "Don't worry," said Tessie Bear. "We just need to go a different way."

Noddy turned the car around and drove back the way he had come. "I promised to pick up Mrs Skittle at three o'clock," he said, " and now I'm going to be so late!" Tessie Bear smiled. "You still have time, Noddy," she told him, gently. "Everything will be fine."

A little way down the road, Noddy spotted Mr Jumbo out jogging. "Ooh, Mr Jumbo does look hot and thirsty," he said as they passed. "Noddy, watch out!" exclaimed Tessie Bear. Noddy was so busy looking at Mr Jumbo that his car went off the road into a field.

Before Noddy could brake, SPLASH! His car sank into a pond. "Now look!" he cried. "We'll definitely never make it to the station now!" "You told Bumpy not to give up, remember?" Tessie Bear pointed out. "Try to think of a way to get us out of this pond."

The little bell on Noddy's hat jingle-jinged as he had an idea. "Can you help us, Mr Jumbo?" he called. Mr Jumbo hurried over and dropped his trunk into the pond. With a long SLU-U-URP he sucked up all the water. "I needed a big drink!" he chuckled.

Now that the pond was empty, Noddy could simply drive out of it. "Thank you, Mr Jumbo!" he called to his friend. "I'm glad I could help," replied Mr Jumbo, waving goodbye. Noddy and Tessie Bear were on their way back to Toy Town again.

It wasn't long before Noddy stopped once more. "Oh, dear," he sighed. "I've forgotten how to get back this way. We're stuck again!" Bumpy Dog jumped out of the car and ran up to a signpost, barking at Noddy to follow. "Well done, Bumpy!" said Tessie Bear.

Noddy set off in the right direction at last and they reached Toy Town Station just in time. "Look, Noddy," said Tessie Bear. "There's Mrs Skittle now. I knew we'd make it!" Mrs Skittle smiled and waved to Noddy, pleased that her taxi had arrived on time.

Noddy stopped to let out Tessie Bear and Bumpy Dog. "Wait there while I take Mrs Skittle home," he told them, "I shan't be long." Mrs Skittle said hello to Noddy as she got into the car and they set off. He soon returned with a surprise for Tessie Bear.

"Oh, Noddy!" exclaimed Tessie Bear, taking the bouquet of pretty flowers from him. "What are these for?" "They're my way of saying thank you," Noddy explained, "for teaching me today that whatever happens, I should never give up!"

BUMPY DOG, FETCH!

Noddy has thrown another stick for Bumpy Dog. Which path should Bumpy Dog follow to fetch it? The answer is at the bottom of the page.

1 2 3

20

CHEW CHEW

Bumpy Dog has fetched his stick and is now giving it a good chew! Use a pencil to practise writing the names of these other things that Bumpy Dog likes to chew on.

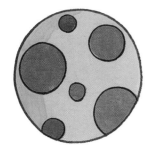

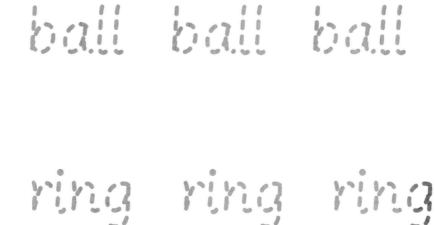

ball ball ball

ring ring ring

shoe shoe shoe

bone bone bone

NODDY'S BUSY DAY

Noddy awakes at seven o'clock,
At eight he leaves the house;
By nine he has a passenger:
It's little Clockwork Mouse!

He drives his friend down to the shops,
At ten he has a snack;
He visits Big-Ears at eleven o'clock,
At twelve he hurries back.

Noddy has some lunch at one,
Then visits Tessie Bear;
He walks with Bumpy Dog at two,
Then drives to the Town Square.

Next he picks up Dinah Doll
To take her home for three;
He cleans his car at four o'clock,
At five, it's time for tea!

NODDY'S ON TIME

Noddy was just in time to pick up Mrs Skittle from the station in the story. Fill in the missing numbers on this clock and say what time Noddy had to be at the station. If you can't remember, have a peep back at the story! When you know the answer, draw the small hand in at the right time on the clock and write down your answer in the space underneath.

Noddy had to be at the station at ………… o'clock.

A YUMMY PICNIC

Noddy is out for another picnic with Tessie Bear and Bumpy Dog. He does not have to rush back to Toy Town this time! If you can find some round-ended scissors, you can help Noddy to put out the picnic things.

Ask a grown-up to help photocopy or trace this page first, then cut out the picnic things. Stick them on to the picnic blanket with paper glue to make a yummy feast!

NODDY AND THE BROKEN CLOCK!

Each day, a little before twelve o'clock, everyone in Toy Town would stop what they were doing and head for the Town Hall; something special happened there at midday. "Hello, Clockwork Mouse!" called Noddy, as he hurried towards the square one morning.

"Hello, Noddy!" replied Clockwork Mouse, before trotting ahead. "Make way!" boomed Mr Plod's voice. "Officer of the law coming through!" Mr Jumbo watched as Mr Plod strode after Noddy. "Has Noddy done something wrong, Mr Plod?" he asked.

"Of course not," Mr Plod replied. "I'm not chasing Noddy, I'm hurrying because it's almost twelve o'clock." Mr Jumbo was surprised. "Goodness, I didn't realise the time!" he chuckled. "We'd better hurry, we don't want to miss our favourite time of the day!"

Mr Jumbo bustled along with the rest of the crowd and they chattered excitedly as they gathered around what they had come to see: the town clock. "It won't be long now!" said Dinah Doll. "I don't know what all the fuss is about," sneered Gobbo goblin.

The crowd fell silent as the clock struck twelve. Everyone counted each chime: "One… two…three…four…five…six…seven…eight…nine…ten…eleven…TWELVE!" They smiled as a clockwork robber popped out of the doors, chased by a clockwork policeman.

The people of Toy Town clapped as the figures disappeared and the clock's doors snapped shut. "It does more than tick-tick-tock, how we love our Toy Town clock!" sang Noddy. "That is a good rhyme, Noddy," said Dinah. "See you the same time tomorrow!"

When Noddy and his friends gathered the next day at noon, they were in for quite a surprise. The clock had barely chimed once before SPROING! Springs and cogs flew out over the crowd and the clock's hands fell loosely downwards. Everybody let out a gasp.

"The clock's broken!" exclaimed Mr Plod. "Fetch Mr Sparks!" Mr Sparks was soon up his ladder, looking at the clock. "Noddy, please pass my special wrench," he called down. Noddy threw the tool a little too far. "Ouch!" yelped Mr Sparks, as it grazed his head.

Rubbing his head, Mr Sparks set to work on the clock as the crowd watched from below. "I'll have this mended in two shakes of a jiffy!" he called down between all the knocking and hammering. He stood back to see if he was right. "Oh, no!" everyone cried.

Mr Sparks scratched his head and wondered how he could get the clockwork figures working properly again. He knocked and hammered into the evening, but it was no use. He tried to please the waiting crowd by chasing the robber past the clock himself.

"You're not a policeman, Mr Sparks!" boomed Mr Plod. Mr Sparks sighed helplessly. "Maybe he can't fix the clock at all!" sniggered Gobbo. "Mr Sparks can fix the clock!" Noddy scolded the goblin. "Mr Sparks can fix anything." Noddy's friends agreed.

Noddy went to see if he could help Mr Sparks. "I just can't make this clock work the way it used to, Noddy," sighed Mr Sparks. "Well, if you can't make it work the old way," said Noddy, "why don't you make it work a different way? We could have a new clock!"

Mr Sparks said Noddy's idea was very good indeed. He asked the people of Toy Town to bring some new parts for him to use in the clock. "Are you sure this will work?" Mr Plod asked, giving Noddy an old handlebar. "Mr Sparks says it will," replied Noddy brightly.

At last the clock was ready. Mr Sparks put the hands to twelve o'clock and it began to chime just as it used to. The clockwork policeman chased the clockwork robber again, but this time fireworks fizzed and banged from the clock to light up the evening sky.

The crowd was delighted. "You'll have to reset the clock to the right time," Mr Plod pointed out, "and we'll have to have our clock show at night now…but well done! You fixed the clock!" Mr Sparks smiled at Noddy and said: "We ALL fixed the clock!"

MR. SPARKS' IS BUSY

Mr Sparks has work to do:
Bits to saw and bobs to glue,
Clocks to look at, trucks to fix,
Nails to hammer, paint to mix,
Nuts to tighten, tanks to fill,
Wheels to change and holes to drill,
Tyres to blow up, cars to test…
Mr Sparks, you need a rest!

'S' IS FOR SPARKS

Mr Sparks' name begins with the 's' sound. Can you spot five other things in the picture that begin with the 's' sound? Draw a circle round each one. The answers are at the bottom of the page.

Answers: a saw, a spanner, a screwdriver, a sponge, a sandwich.

MR. SPARKS' SPANNERS

Noddy's aeroplane needs mending and Mr Sparks has come to see what the problem is.
One of the tools that Mr Sparks might use is a spanner. See if you can find the five spanners hidden in the picture. Once you have found them all, use your crayons or pencils to colour the picture.

LIE DOWN, MR WOBBLY MAN!

It was Mr Wobbly Man's birthday. His friends were having a tea party for him in the town square and Tessie Bear had made lots of delicious treats to eat. Mr Wobbly Man happily rocked to and fro, chuckling with delight and thanking everyone for his presents.

Soon it was time for the birthday cake. Everyone sang 'Happy Birthday' and Mr Wobbly Man wobbled backwards as he took a deep breath. Quickly swinging forwards, he blew as hard as he could and his special Mr Wobbly Man candle wobbled before going out.

"Ooh, eating all that food has made me tired," yawned Noddy, flopping down on the grass. Tessie Bear sat next to him and glanced up. "Look, Noddy," she smiled, "the clouds are perfect today!" They both laid back and tried to spot funny shapes in the sky.

"That cloud looks like Gobbo!" giggled Noddy. Tessie Bear spotted the goblin cloud and pointed to the one next to it. "That one looks like Sly," she added, "and the next one looks like Mr Plod's hat. Perhaps those naughty goblins have taken it as a trick!"

"Come and lie down next to us, Mr Wobbly Man!" called Noddy. "We can see funny clouds in the sky!" Mr Wobbly Man picked up a basket and rocked backwards with it on his chest. He hoped it would help him to stay down, but he popped straight back up again.

"It's no good," Mr Wobbly Man sighed. "I've never been able to lie down." "But how do you sleep?" Noddy asked, puzzled. Mr Wobbly Man showed him: he rocked back and forth, back and forth. "But it would be nice to lie down just once," he added sadly.

Noddy said they would find a way to make Mr Wobbly Man lie down. It was his birthday, after all! They watched as Bumpy Dog knocked the skittle children in all directions. The little skittles loved falling over. "Down we go!" they laughed.

"That's it!" cried Noddy, with a jingle-jing of his hat. "Let's get Bumpy Dog to help!" Tessie Bear called Bumpy over and told him to give Mr Wobbly Man a big birthday bump. "Woof! Woof!" he barked, leaping up and knocking Mr Wobbly Man backwards.

"Whoah!" chuckled Mr Wobbly Man, seeing the sky at last. "Hooray!" cheered Noddy and Tessie Bear. Bumpy Dog balanced on Mr Wobbly Man for a moment, but Mr Wobbly Man's wobble was too strong for him and he yelped as he was thrown off again.

"We need a better idea," said Tessie Bear. Noddy's bell tinkled again as he thought of something. He trotted off and came back with the Bouncing Balls. They bounced all at once on to Mr Wobbly Man to try and keep him down. "Ouch! Yow!" he cried. "Stop!"

"Thank you very much for trying to help, Bouncing Balls," said Mr Wobbly Man, "but that hurts too much. I suppose I shall never see the clouds." Even before all the balls had bounced away, Noddy's bell rang and he dashed off to Dinah Doll's stall for a mirror.

Noddy gave the mirror to his friend. "I can see myself," smiled Mr Wobbly Man. "Happy birthday, me! Now, if I turn the mirror this way…I can see the clouds! How wonderful!" Mr Wobbly Man wobbled along, looking at the sky in his new mirror.

Mr Wobbly Man was so busy gazing at the funny clouds that he wasn't paying attention to where he was going. "Ho, ho! That cloud looks just like a…YOW!" he cried, bumping into a lamp-post and dropping his mirror. "Oh!" he sighed, disappointed. "It's broken."

"Are you all right, Mr Wobbly Man?" asked Noddy and Tessie Bear. "Yes, thank you," replied their friend, rubbing his sore nose. "I'm just fed up with being different. All I want is to see the clouds once." Noddy smiled. He could help Mr Wobbly Man!

Noddy took Mr Wobbly Man for a ride in his aeroplane. "Now you can see the clouds!" he chuckled. "Look!" Mr Wobbly Man pointed excitedly. "That one looks like a rabbit! And that one looks like ME! Oh, Noddy, thank you…this is the best birthday ever!"

FUNNY CLOUDS

In the story, Mr Wobbly Man was delighted to see a cloud shaped just like him! Use your pencil to match each funny cloud to a Toy Town friend.

MR WOBBLY MAN IS WOBBLY

There once was a round man call Wobbly,
Who went down a street that was cobbly.
He swayed to and fro
And cried out, "Oh, no!
I must find a way that's less knobbly!"

Use your crayons or pencils to colour the picture of wobbly Mr Wobbly Man.

BRING ON THE CLOUDS

Noddy is taking Mr Wobbly Man out cloud spotting again. Use your pencils to draw lots of funny clouds for them to look at. Clouds come in all shapes and sizes, so you can make them whatever shape you like!

SKY HIGH

You often see clouds in the sky, and sometimes you might see Noddy up there in his aeroplane, too! Which of these things belong up in the sky? Which one would you never see in the sky? Where would you normally see it?

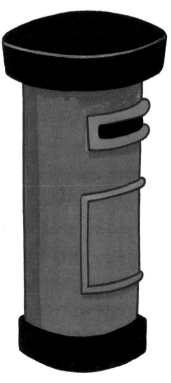

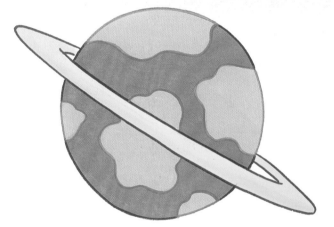

 49

I LOVE MY BED

It's where I wake up
In the morning;
It's where I go
When I start yawning.
Its sheets are cool
When I am hot;
It has warm blankets
For when I'm not.

I'll rest there after
A hard day,
Or if I'm ill,
It's where I'll stay.
I'll lie there now
To read a book…
Which story next?
Let's take a look!

NODDY'S BEDTIME STORIES

Stop, Noddy, Stop!
Driving Miss Pink Cat
Noddy On The Move

STOP, NODDY, STOP!

Noddy and Bumpy Dog were delivering parcels around Toy Town one morning, when Noddy's car began to make a funny noise: SSSFUMP!

"That doesn't sound right, little car," Noddy frowned.

"Woof! Woof!" agreed Bumpy Dog.

"Parp! Parp!" agreed the car.

"When we've delivered this parcel," Noddy added, "we'll go and see Mr Sparks."

Mr Sparks waved and smiled when he saw Noddy driving into the garage. He asked what the problem was and Noddy explained the funny sssfumpy noise.

"Ah, I know what that is," nodded Mr Sparks, peering under the car's bonnet. "I'll mend your car this afternoon and you can pick it up at teatime."

Noddy thanked
Mr Sparks and
began to walk home
with Bumpy Dog.
"Hello, Big-Ears," he called, spotting
his friend riding past. Big-Ears
stopped and asked Noddy where
his car was.
"Mr Sparks is mending it," Noddy explained. "I shall have to do
without it until teatime."
"Well, hop on to my bicycle," smiled Big-Ears. "You can come to my Toadstool House
for a spot of lunch while you're waiting."

Big-Ears made a tasty lunch and the two friends talked about what was going on in Toy Town while Bumpy Dog snuffled around in Toadstool Wood.

"Come on, Bumpy!" Noddy called when it was time to leave. He and Big-Ears climbed aboard the bicycle and set off. Still Bumpy Dog didn't come.

"Bumpy!" shouted Noddy. "Come on, or you'll get left behind!" He looked back to see Bumpy chasing away Sly and Gobbo, the naughty goblins.

"Bumpy Dog has found someone to play with," Noddy giggled. They waited for him to come bounding up and headed back to Toy Town.

Big-Ears stopped at Dinah Doll's stall to buy one or two things.
"Can I borrow your bicycle for a moment, Big-Ears?" asked Noddy.
"What for?" replied Big-Ears.
"It's a surprise," Noddy smiled.
"Very well," agreed Big-Ears, "as long as you're careful with it."
Noddy wanted to buy Big-Ears a big ice cream for being so kind.
He pedalled off to Miss Pink Cat's ice cream parlour and left the
bicycle outside. After buying a huge Googleberry Surprise, he set
off back to the market with it. Mr Jumbo also came
out to get on his bicycle and was astonished
to see Big-Ears' bicycle in its place.
"Noddy, stop!" he called. "You have the
wrong bicycle."

Noddy looked back, but
did not hear what Mr
Jumbo was
saying.
"Oh, dear," he
thought. "Mr
Jumbo looks cross
with me...but I
haven't done
anything
wrong!"

BUMP

SPLAT

"Stop, Noddy, stop!"

Mr Jumbo called out again and began to give chase. Instead of stopping, Noddy panicked and pedalled even faster. He rode as fast as he could to the market and BUMP! He went straight into Dinah Doll's stall, knocking things over and covering them with ice cream.

"Noddy!" gasped Dinah. "What are you doing?"

"And what have you done with my bicycle?" asked Big-Ears crossly.

"I don't think it's damaged," groaned Noddy, getting up.

"I don't think it's my bicycle!" his friend exclaimed.

"No, it's mine," panted Mr Jumbo, trotting up. "Noddy, you took it by mistake."

Poor Noddy said sorry to Mr Jumbo and gave back his bicycle. Then he said sorry to Dinah Doll, helping to pick up the things he had knocked over and clean the ice cream off them. Finally, he said sorry to Big-Ears for leaving his bicycle behind and walked back to the ice cream parlour to get it. He had to buy another Googleberry Surprise, too.

"Thank you, Noddy," said Big-Ears, taking his ice cream and getting his bicycle back at last. "And next time someone tells you to stop, you must stop, Noddy, stop!"

DRIVING MISS PINK CAT

It was a hot day in Toyland and the Ice Cream Parlour was very busy.
"Mmm, your milk shakes are the best," Noddy told Miss Pink Cat.
"Thank you," Miss Pink Cat smiled. "Noddy," she added, "how would you like to have all the ice cream you can eat?"
"I'd love it!" gasped Noddy. Miss Pink Cat told Noddy that she would give him ice cream in return for being her driver. Noddy explained that his little taxi was supposed to be for everyone, but with all the talk of chocolate milk shakes and googleberry sundaes, he agreed. His first job was to collect a special order from Dinah Doll's stall, so he drove to the market.

"Hello, Dinah Doll," said Noddy. "Miss Pink Cat has sent me to pick up her special something."

"Ah, yes. Here it is." Dinah Doll handed Noddy a new handkerchief.

"One handkerchief?" Noddy looked puzzled.

"Miss Pink Cat always buys them one at a time," chuckled Dinah Doll.

Noddy delivered the handkerchief, hoping for a big googleberry sundae. But Miss Pink Cat wanted him to drive her to the Town Square.

"The Town Square is only there," Noddy said, pointing.

"If I wanted to walk, I wouldn't have a driver," sniffed Miss Pink Cat. "Drive me now, please, and open the door for me while you're about it."

Noddy was beginning to wish he had not said he would work for Miss Pink Cat, but he opened the door for her and drove the short distance to the Town Square.

"Mind the bumps!" Miss Pink Cat snapped on the way. She told Noddy to wait, then returned and made him drive back to the Ice Cream Parlour.

"Perhaps now I could have a big bowl of…" Noddy began.

"No, no," Miss Pink Cat interrupted. "You must get me a new hankie first. This one is wrinkled."

Noddy complained to Dinah about his new job.

"Miss Pink Cat is a little…fussy," Dinah agreed. "But she wouldn't want you as her driver if you didn't do it so well."

Noddy's hat jingle-jinged as he had an idea: he would drive badly, then Miss Pink Cat would not want him as her driver anymore!

The next time Miss Pink Cat told Noddy to go around a bump, he did just that…and went back the way they had come.

"Noddy, what are you doing?" asked Miss Pink Cat, crossly.

"You told me to go around the bump," smiled Noddy. Miss Pink Cat told him to turn, so he steered the car on to the grass.

"You can't drive on the grass!" exclaimed Miss Pink Cat. "Stop it!"

Noddy stopped the car.

"You said stop it," he said with a shrug. Miss Pink Cat lost her temper and said she would drive. Just as she sat in the driver's seat, Mr Plod appeared.

"Miss Pink Cat," he said, sternly, "you should know better than to drive on the grass."

"But…I mean…" stuttered Miss Pink Cat.

"May I see your driving licence?" Mr Plod asked. As Miss Pink Cat did not have one, she had to go with him to the police station.

"Should I come and wait outside for you?" Noddy asked.

"No!" Miss Pink Cat snapped, as she got out and slammed the door. "I never want to get in a car with you again!"

After talking to Mr Plod, Miss Pink Cat agreed that she was being unfair and said sorry to Noddy. Noddy went to tell Dinah Doll.

"You haven't come for another hankie, have you?" she smiled.

"No," Noddy replied. "I am driving for everyone again, not just Miss Pink Cat. She does owe me some ice cream, though."

"How much?" asked Dinah.

"More than both of us can eat," said Noddy. "So come with me to the Ice Cream Parlour and have some. I'll even drive you there!"

NODDY ON THE MOVE

Noddy loved books; he had just read a story about a sailor's adventures.

"It must be exciting being a sailor, always moving to new places," he said to Master Tubby Bear.

"Why don't you move somewhere else, Noddy?" asked Master Tubby Bear. "You could move to the airport and fly your aeroplane more often. Vroooom!"

Noddy giggled as Master Tubby Bear ran around with his arms out, pretending to be an aeroplane.

"Or I could live by the Ice Cream Parlour," Noddy added, "and have a Googleberry Surprise whenever I liked. What a good idea. Master Tubby Bear, I'm going to find a better place to live and you can help me!"

Noddy decided to move that very day. He did not need to pack: he simply hooked his house to his little car so that he could tow it along. "Noddy, what on earth are you doing?" asked Big-Ears, as the friends set off.

"I'm going to find the perfect place to live," Noddy replied.
"And I'm helping," added Master Tubby Bear.

"I thought you were happy here," said Big-Ears.

"I'll be even happier somewhere else," smiled Noddy. "Goodbye, Big-Ears."

CLUCK

CLUCK
CLUCK
CLUCK

Noddy decided that Tessie Bear would be a good neighbour and parked his house next to hers.

"We can have tea and cakes together every day," said Tessie Bear, delighted. But it wasn't long before her chickens made themselves at home in Noddy's House-For-One.

"I can't have chickens scratching around my house!" Noddy gasped.

"Well, you are on their favourite spot," Tessie Bear pointed out. Noddy did not want to share his house with clucking chickens, so he said goodbye to Tessie Bear and towed his house away.

Noddy often had to take his car to Toy Town garage to be mended, so he thought it would be a good idea to live there with Mr Sparks. He had just made some tea when he was startled by a noise so loud that it shook the house.

"W-what's th-that?" he asked, carefully putting down the teapot.

"Mr Sparks is using some machinery," Master Tubby Bear explained. "It's quite loud, isn't it?"

"Noddy!" shouted Mr Sparks from outside. "Please move your house, I need to get the tow truck out soon."

Noddy sighed and decided to try living in the Town Square.

"This is better," he smiled, once there. "And I shall always have a friend nearby. There's someone knocking at the door now!"

It was Mr Jumbo. He came inside and began to unpack a basket of food.

"I always have a picnic here," he told Noddy. "Your house is in the way, so I shall have to eat it inside today."

BOING BOING BOING

While Noddy waited politely for Mr Jumbo to finish his picnic, he heard another noise: BOUNCE! GIGGLE! BOING! It was the Bouncing Balls bouncing around the house.

"Why are those balls doing that?" asked Noddy.

"They practise here every day," Mr Jumbo replied. "Your house being here won't stop them."

Noddy stood in his doorway, frowning at the balls leaping to and fro.

"Move in the name of Plod!" boomed Mr Plod, striding up.

"But I've just got here," Noddy protested. Mr Plod shook his head.

"The Town Square is for picnicking and bouncing and special occasions," he said, sternly. "Move along, please."

Noddy and Master Tubby Bear asked Big-Ears where they should go next.
"I know a place that you will definitely like," Big-Ears smiled knowingly. "It's a nice, quiet spot with no Bouncing Balls and no chickens."
"Where is it, Big-Ears?" asked Noddy excitedly. "Where, where, where?"
Big-Ears led the two friends through Toy Town...straight back to where Noddy used to live!
"Oh, Big-Ears," chuckled Noddy. "You're right. Why do I need to move when I already have the perfect place to live? This is my home, sweet home...and it always will be!"

SLEEPY TIME

I've watched the moon and seen it rise,
Now I ought to close my eyes…
Just one more look at the night sky,
In case a shooting star goes by.
I'd like to gaze up there all night
And stay awake until daylight,
But sleep I must, or I will be
A very grumpy, tired Noddy!

ICE-COLD TREATS

Miss Pink Cat has served Noddy and Dinah Doll with Ice Cream Parlour specials to make up for treating Noddy so badly. She thinks she has put out two of everything, but there is one thing missing. Match up the pairs to find out what she has given to both friends and draw a circle round the odd one out.

71

THERE'S NO PLACE LIKE HOME

I want to move from here, I really do!
I'm sure to be much happier somewhere new…
I'll pull my house along
While I sing a merry song
And Master Tubby Bear will help me, too.

We find a lovely spot at Tessie Bear's
And for a while we don't have any cares,
Until the hens come in –
My goodness! What a din!
And those sharp claws are ruining my chairs!

The Town Square? Well, that seems to be as bad,
With picnickers and balls bouncing like mad.
We go back to the start
To a place special in my heart:
I'm in my home, sweet home and I'm so glad!

TOO MANY CHICKENS

Look at these things from the story about Noddy moving house. Say how many there are of each and use a pencil to practise writing the numbers.

1 1 1 1 1 1

2 2 2 2 2

3 3 3 3 3

4 4 4 4 4

5 5 5 5 5

WHOSE HOUSE?

Noddy tried moving his House-For-One to a new place, but he would never leave it altogether! Use a pencil to join up Noddy and his little house, then match his Toy Town friends to their homes.

NODDY, THE BEST DRIVER IN THE WORLD

Sometimes Noddy used his aeroplane to deliver parcels, but often he would fly just because he liked to! One morning, he was weaving through the clouds in his aeroplane when Martha Monkey spotted him. "Oooh, that looks fun!" she said, as she watched.

When Noddy landed his aeroplane, Martha Monkey ran up to him. "Noddy!" she called excitedly. "Can I fly your aeroplane? Please can I?" Noddy smiled and shook his head. "I'm sorry, Martha, but you don't know how to. It's too dangerous." Martha was cross.

"Just because you fly a plane and drive a car doesn't make you the best driver in the world," she snapped. "I once drove three things in one day." "Well, I can drive four things," Noddy retorted. "I can drive five," said Martha. "Six!" "Seven!" "EIGHT!"

Martha said Noddy had to prove that he could drive eight different things before the day was out. "If not, you have to teach me to fly your aeroplane," she added. Noddy climbed out of his aeroplane and drove his car a little way. "That's two things already!" he called.

Noddy stopped his car and wondered what he could drive next. "Easy!" he said, spotting the airport's fire engine nearby and running over to it. "Isn't that too big for you?" asked Martha. "No! Just watch," replied Noddy, before driving the fire engine with ease.

Noddy parked the fire engine and jumped down from it. "Hmm, what else can I drive?" he said. "You'll never think of five more things!" Martha giggled. "Yes, I will," sang Noddy, smiling as he saw puffs of steam in the distance. "I've seen the next one already!"

Noddy drove Martha to Toy Town Station and they went on to the platform. Noddy asked the driver if he could steer the Toyland Express for a few minutes and they were soon chuff-chuffing along. "That's four things, Martha!" Noddy called back cheerily.

Back at the station, Noddy wondered: "Now, what other things go?" His little bell rang. "Go! That's it!" he exclaimed, driving to his house. He trotted over to his go-cart and pedalled it down the road. "This is fun, Martha!" he chuckled. "And it's number five!"

Noddy went to see if Mr Sparks could help with vehicle number six. "I could lend you my tow-truck," offered Mr Sparks. "That's very kind of you, thank you," said Noddy. Martha sighed as he rumbled past, calling: "I think that brings me up to number six!"

Noddy jumped down from the tow-truck and smiled at Martha. "You still have to think of two more things," she reminded him. "I know. There's something!" exclaimed Noddy, pointing to a horse-drawn cart nearby. "There's something," Martha agreed, glumly.

Noddy asked if he could borrow the cart for a moment and clambered up to drive it. "Giddy up!" he called, flicking the reins. "Well, Martha, that's number seven!" he added brightly, as the cart trundled along. "Please don't remind me," replied Martha.

Noddy could not think of one more thing to drive. "It looks as if you're going to have to teach me to fly your aeroplane after all!" chuckled Martha. "Help me think of something," said Noddy. "Please, Martha!" Mr Plod came over to see the two friends.

When Noddy saw Mr Plod, his hat jingle-jinged. "Of course!" he exclaimed. "Mr Plod, please may I ride your bicycle for a moment?" Mr Plod looked puzzled, but agreed. "Martha, I did it!" sang Noddy, riding round in a circle. "I drove eight things in one day!"

Noddy gave back Mr Plod's bicycle and the two friends said goodbye to him.
"Aw…now I'll never get to fly your aeroplane," sighed Martha. "Maybe not," smiled
Noddy, "but I could take you for a ride in it." Martha was delighted. "Really?" she
asked eagerly.

The sun was beginning to set as Noddy took off in his aeroplane with Martha. "The
day's almost over," said Noddy. "I only just managed to drive eight things!" Martha
stretched her arms out. "Wheeee!" she cried. "Noddy, you are the best driver in the
world!"

WHICH WHEELS?

Do you remember the fourth thing with wheels that Noddy drove in the story? Join the dots to find the answer, then use your crayons or pencils to colour the rest of the picture.

FOUR WHEEL FUN

Here are some of the things with wheels that Noddy rode in the story. Use a pencil to draw a circle round the odd one out in each row.

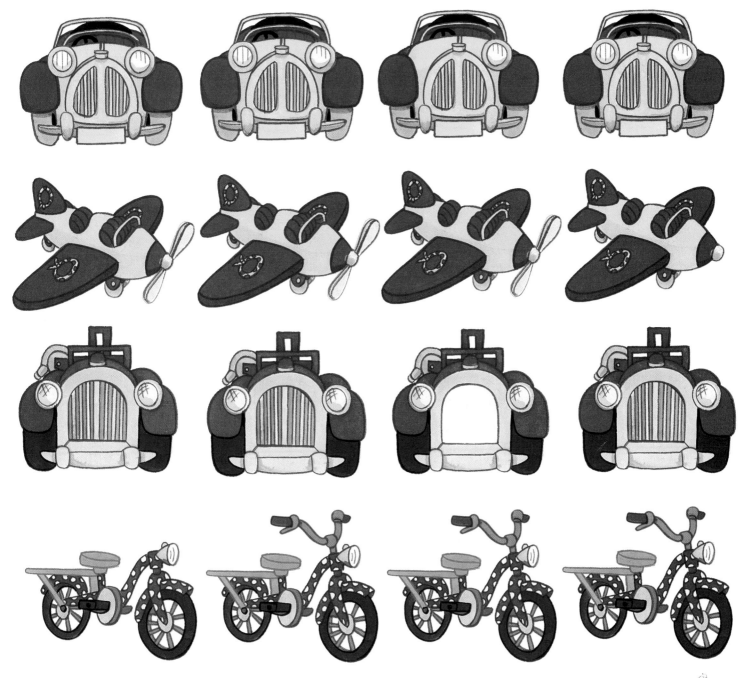

85

THE BEST DRIVER

I'm the world's best driver -
Now Martha knows I am!
It doesn't even bother me
If there's a traffic jam.

As long as I am driving,
I'm happy as can be.
A car, a truck, a go-cart:
They all seem fun to me!

My favourite is my aeroplane,
I love to fly up high.
Sometimes I take a passenger
And show them round the sky!

MAKING TRACKS

Things with wheels leave all sorts of different tracks. Use your pencil to match each vehicle with the marks it leaves behind!

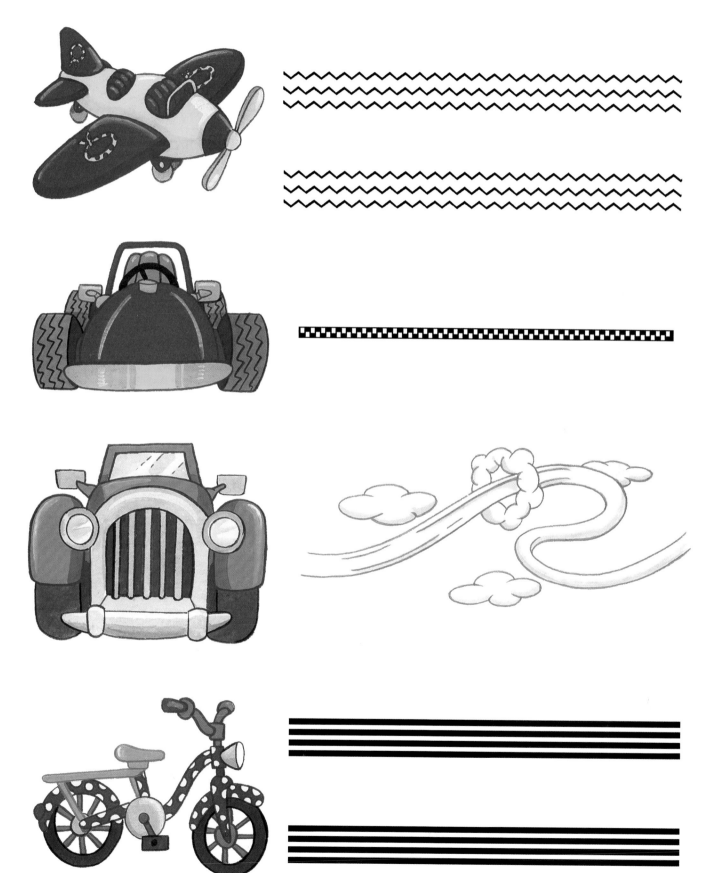

TOY TOWN TRAFFIC

Noddy has had a busy day in his little taxi and now it is time for him to go back to his House-For-One for tea. He will pass lots of things with wheels on his way home! Count up how many fire engines, tractors, cars, bikes and tow trucks he will see and use a pencil to write your answers in the boxes.

NODDY AND THE MAGIC RUBBER

Noddy was very busy. His car was full of parcels that needed delivering all over Toy Town. As he drove along the road, Master Tubby Bear stuck out his arm. "Noddy, please stop!" he called. "I need a ride home!" Noddy pulled his car into the kerb.

"Sorry, Master Tubby Bear," said Noddy, "but my car is full of parcels." Master Tubby Bear took a parcel from the front seat. "Leave this here while you take me," he suggested. "No, no, no!" exclaimed Noddy, pulling back the parcel. "That's for Big-Ears."

Noddy said he would come back for Master Tubby Bear and drove away. Left behind was something that looked like a rubber. Master Tubby Bear picked it up. "I think this dropped out of Big-Ears' parcel," he said, peering at it. "How did that happen?"

"It must have rubbed a hole in its box," he grinned. "It must be magic!" Mr Jumbo was painting in the park nearby. He looked up from his picture and gasped. "Where's my picnic lunch gone?" he asked. Master Tubby Bear giggled: he had rubbed it out!

Meanwhile, Big-Ears had opened his parcel. "It's a new art kit," he smiled. "Thank you, Noddy. Oh!" He noticed a hole in the box. "The magic rubber is missing. It probably fell out of here." Noddy knew Master Tubby Bear must have it. "I'll find it," he promised.

As Noddy drove back from Toadstool Wood, Master Tubby Bear looked for someone else to play a trick on. He saw Dinah Doll and Tessie Bear enjoying some googleberry muffins. "Good afternoon," Mr Plod said as he passed. "Good afternoon!" they replied.

Dinah Doll turned back to the plate. "I knew you were hungry, Tessie Bear," she gasped, "but you didn't have to eat all the muffins." "I didn't!" Tessie Bear protested, seeing the empty plate. "You must have eaten them!" Master Tubby Bear chuckled to himself.

When Mr Plod reached the police station, he thought the door was open. "Hmm, I'm sure I shut it earlier," he said, stepping into the doorway. He saw that the door was not open but had, in fact, disappeared. "Who would want to steal my door?" wondered Mr Plod.

Master Tubby Bear was wondering what he could rub out next when Sly and Gobbo appeared next to him. "I see you have a magic rubber," said Gobbo. "We could use it to take whatever we want. Some ice-creams, perhaps, or maybe even a tow-truck…"

Master Tubby Bear frowned. "That would be stealing," he said. "No, I shall keep this in my pocket where you two can't reach it." He walked away from the goblins, but the magic rubber rubbed a hole in his pocket and dropped out. Gobbo grinned as he saw it.

"Master Tubby Bear, you've dropped your…" began Sly. "Ssssh!" hissed Gobbo, scrambling to pick up the rubber. They both peered at it. "Now we've got what we wanted," sniggered Gobbo. "We can get into any building in Toy Town!"

Noddy found Master Tubby Bear. "Have you seen the rubber that fell out of Big-Ears' parcel?" he asked. Master Tubby Bear fidgeted a little and admitted that he had. "Master Tubby Bear! You shouldn't touch things that don't belong to you!" Noddy scolded.

"I know," said Master Tubby Bear. "I put it in my pocket so the goblins…oh!" He felt the hole in his empty pocket. "If Sly and Gobbo have it, there'll be trouble, trouble, trouble," warned Noddy. He began to smile as his hat jingle-jinged and he had an idea.

The goblins decided they would use the magic rubber to get ice-creams. They crept up to the ice-cream parlour and rubbed a hole in the wall. "Uh-oh!" exclaimed Gobbo. Inside was Mr Plod. He came over to the goblins and took the rubber. "Thank you," he said.

Sly and Gobbo were put behind bars, while Master Tubby Bear went to give Big-Ears his rubber. "What a good idea to make the police station look like the ice-cream parlour," said Mr Plod. Noddy smiled, calling to the goblins: "No more vanishing tricks for you!"

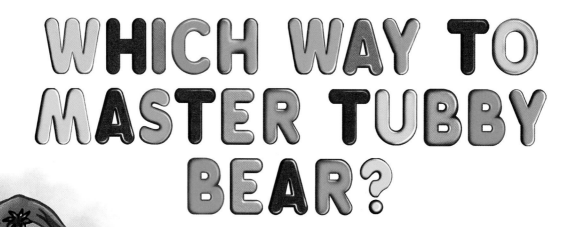

WHICH WAY TO MASTER TUBBY BEAR?

Noddy is looking for Master Tubby Bear to ask him what has happened to Big-Ears' magic rubber. Use a pencil or your finger to show Noddy which way to go!

MUFFIN MAGIC

Do you remember how Master Tubby Bear made the googleberry muffins disappear in the story? Use your pens or pencils to draw some more muffins for Dinah Doll and Tessie Bear. Don't forget the purple googleberries!

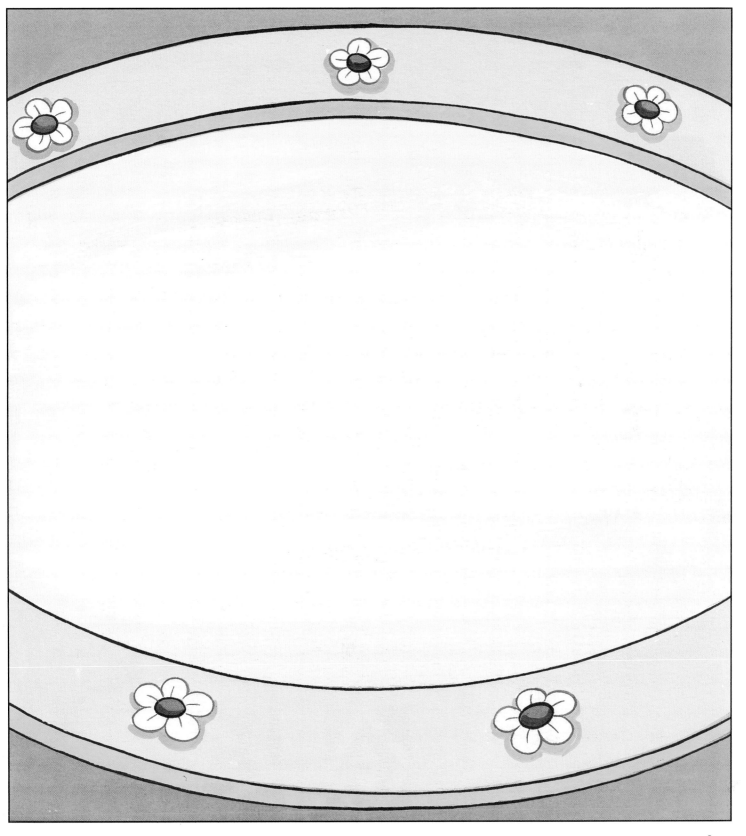

THE MAGIC MIRROR

Noddy found a looking glass
he knew he mustn't touch,
But seeing his reflection in it
made him laugh so much,
He had to hold on to the frame,
which made the glass go odd;
Noddy found he could step through
and saw stern Mr Plod,

Running Dinah's market stall,
while goblins ran the town;
Dinah mended cars and trucks
and ducks swam upside down!
"This is wrong! It's not Toy Town!"
little Noddy cried,

He ran to find the looking glass
and stepped right back inside.
"That was Topsy-Turvy Town!"
he gasped, back in Toyland.
"From now on I shall look just with
my eyes and not my hands!"

TOPSY TURVY TOWN

Noddy thinks Topsy-Turvy Town is very strange indeed. He can see five topsy-turvy things here! See if you can spot them all and use a pencil to draw a circle round them. The answers are at the bottom of the page.

Answers: The ducks are upside down; Noddy's car is a different colour; there are stars, as well as a sun, in the sky; there is an armchair on the pavement; there is a bush with bells on it.

NODDY'S TRICKY MORNING

Join in this story by saying what the pictures are as they appear.

woke up one morning and looked at his bedside .

"That's funny," he thought. "My says it's time to get

up, but it still looks dark outside." Thinking his must

be fast, went back to sleep. He woke up an hour

later, but it was still dark so he closed his eyes again.

Then he heard the sound of the giggling outside

his . He jumped out of bed and tried to look out, but

the had been painted black. "Those naughty

have played a trick on me!" cried . "Now I'm late!"

quickly got ready and had breakfast, before dashing

to his car.  was standing there with the . "I caught these two lurking outside your house," he said sternly. "Is everything all right, ?" "Actually, , I'm late for my first passenger," replied . "The put black paint on my so that I would think it was still dark." "Did they now?" said , turning to the sheepish . "We shall have to make sure they don't do it again, shan't we?" made the clean the paint off Noddy's . "Now you must clean every in Toy Town," he told them. "Don't look so glum about it," giggled to the miserable , as he drove away. "You should be finished by tea time!"

A WACKY WHISTLE

Sly and Gobbo have changed Mr Plod's whistle for a trick one that honks. They are going to be in big trouble when he catches them! Look at the two pictures and draw a circle round each of the five differences in the second one. The answers are at the bottom of the page.

Answers: 1. Star on Plod's helmet 2. Plod's hand 3. The sun 4. Plod's nose 5. Sly's hat

A SQUIRTY SURPRISE

"What shall we do? Play a trick?"
Asked Gobbo one day in his house.
"There are plenty," Sly said, "take your pick.
A sweet that tastes yucky? A mouse?"

Gobbo wrapped up a nice flower
And sent it to poor Tessie Bear.
It arrived and then gave her a shower,
She cried, "Oh, that's really not fair!"

Mr Plod marched the pair to the shop
To buy Tessie some blooms that were real.
He said, "These tricks really must stop!
Be good or it's jail, that's the deal."

Tessie Bear took her flowers and was pleased –
It seemed the pair had changed their ways!
"We have changed," the two goblins teased,
"We'll be good…for at least a few days!"

TWO NAUGHTY GOBLINS

Sly and Gobbo are playing another trick on Noddy while he is away from his car.
What do you think they have done? What will happen when Noddy drives away?

Use your crayons or pens to colour the picture of the goblins and Noddy's car. See if you can match the colours to those on the opposite page.

WHERE IS NODDY'S CAR?

While Noddy was having tea with Big-Ears, Sly and Gobbo hid his car. What a naughty trick! Can you see where they left it? Find a dice and counters so that you and a friend or two can take a trip through Toadstool Wood to help Noddy find his car.

1

2

3

4

5

14

13

11

32

10

33

7

9

8

34

35

108

Take a counter for each player and place the counters on the start. Take turns to throw the dice and work your way round Toadstool Wood, making sure you throw a six to start. If you land on a magic toadstool, you can skip on two spaces. If you land on a squirrel, you must miss a go to feed him some nuts! The first one to reach Noddy's car is the winner. Look out for naughty goblins!

15 16 17 19 20 21 22 23

28 27 26 25

29

38 37 39 40